TOPSY AND TIM THURSDAY BOOK

Jean and Gareth Adamson

Blackie

Copyright © 1977 Jean and Gareth Adamson
This edition copyright © Jean and Gareth Adamson

British Library Cataloguing in Publication Data
Adamson, Jean
Topsy and Tim's thursday book
I. Title   II. Adamson, Gareth
823'.914[J]   PZ7

ISBN 0–216–92047–7
ISBN 0–216–92046–9

Blackie and Son Limited
7 Leicester Place
London WC2H 7BP

Printed in Great Britain by
Thomson Litho Ltd, East Kilbride, Scotland

When Topsy and Tim looked out of
the window for the first time on
Thursday morning, they saw Sister
Cowan the midwife arriving in her car.

'Hello, Sister Cowan,' shouted Topsy and Tim. Sister Cowan waved. 'Can't stop now, twins' she called back. 'I'm in a great hurry.' And she walked very quickly into the bungalow next door, where Mr and Mrs Rupert lived.

Dad tied Topsy's bow, and saw that
Tim combed his hair properly.
'Where's Mummy?' asked Topsy.
'She'll be back in time for dinner,'
said Dad. 'We're all on our own till
then, and I want you to be extra
specially good.'

Topsy and Tim ate their breakfast.
Then they helped to dry the dishes.
'I wonder where Mummy is,' said Tim.
'You'll know quite soon,' smiled
Dad. It was all very odd.

'Come along,' said Dad. 'I'll take you to school.'
'We can go by ourselves,' said Tim.
'I'll take you, just the same,'
said Dad, 'on my way to work.'
Topsy and Tim carried Dad's big
briefcase between them.

Topsy and Tim were the first
children at school. 'You are
bright and early!' said Miss
Maypole.
'Our Mummy's gone away,' said
Tim.
Miss Maypole smiled. 'I'm sure
she'll come back,' she said.

Topsy and Tim were the first
children at the classroom door.
And there was Mummy, waiting
to meet them.
'Where have you been, Mummy?'
shouted Topsy and Tim together.
Mummy laughed. 'Not very far
away,' she said.

After dinner, Mummy said, 'I want you to be very good and very quiet.'
'What for?' said Tim, who wanted to make a noise.
'For a nice reason,' said Mummy. 'I will show you soon, if you are good and quiet.'

'Sshh! You mustn't make a noise,'
said Topsy, 'or Mummy won't show
us the nice reason.'
Tim was very good and quiet then.

Topsy and Tim went out to play
in their own little garden plot.
Tim found a fat, wriggling worm.
He began to sing a song about it.

'Topsy! Tim!' called Mummy's
voice. They looked all round,
but they couldn't see her anywhere.

'Here I am!' she laughed. 'In Mrs Rupert's garden.'

Mummy opened the little gate in
the fence and let them through.
They had never been in Mrs Rupert's
garden before. It was very interesting.

'Up on your tip-toes!' said
Mummy. She led them quietly
down the garden path, till they
came to the big bedroom window
of Mrs Rupert's bungalow.
'Who's going to look in first?'
she whispered.
'Won't Mrs Rupert be cross if we
look in her window?' said Tim.
'Not just this once,' said Mummy,
quietly.
She lifted Topsy up. Tim climbed
on to a box.

In Mrs Rupert's bedroom, Sister
Cowan was bending over a new
cot. She lifted a white bundle
from the cot and carried it
close to the window, for Topsy
and Tim to see. A tiny, pink
face was peeping out.
'There!' said Mummy. 'That's
Master Robin Rupert—your new
next-door neighbour.'
Master Robin Rupert began to cry,
very loudly.

When Dad came home, Topsy and Tim told him about their new neighbour. 'He's only *that* big,' laughed Topsy, 'but he cries louder than Tim!'